HOPE

This is dedicated to my sons, Richie and Tyler. Once you came into my life, I realized the true meaning of Hope.— Shaggy

Dedicated to my grandparents, Thelma and Herman Sr. and Virginia and John, and to my parents, Claudia and Joe, and my parents in-law, Dot and Rob. I love you.— JB

ISBN 0-439-38048-0

Text and illustrations copyright © 2003 by ONE GAZILLION, INC.

All rights reserved.   Published by Scholastic Inc., 557 Broadway, New York, NY 10012.
SCHOLASTIC, CARTWHEEL BOOKS, and associated logos are trademarks and/or registered trademarks of Scholastic Inc.

Library of Congress Cataloging-in-Publication Data available

The text type was set in Cathodelic.
Book design by Steven Scott.

12 11 10 9 8 7 6 5 4 3 2 1   03 04 05 06 07

Printed in China   62
First Scholastic printing, February 2003

HOPE

by Shaggy
Illustrated by Joseph Buckingham Jr.

SCHOLASTIC INC.

New York Toronto London Auckland Sydney Mexico City New Delhi Hong Kong Buenos Aires

I remember—wasn't so long ago. . . .

And Mama, by herself, raised me and my bro.

Wasn't easy, but she did it with the little that flowed.

Gave us drive to survive—
really showed us the way.

And the boat may be rocky.
You can cry.

Just never give up,
you can never give up.

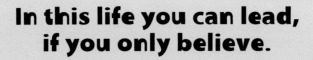

In this life you can lead,
if you only believe.

In order to achieve what you need,

you can never **give** up, you can **never** **give** up.

And it's hope
that keeps me holding on.

It's just hope
that makes me carry on.

Homegrown, couldn't have made it alone.

Now I got a wonderful life, two kids of my own.

With a strong foundation
that was carved in stone.

Thank my mother for the love
that made my house a home.

**Makes me wonder sometimes
if it was meant to be.**

All I ever really wanted was a family.

Teach my kids the same values
that she gave to me.

— Give Thanks —